Includes Compact Disc

W9-AAE-483

CHUCK THE DUCK WAS A COOL DUDE

MAGIC E AND THE LONG U SOUND

By BLAKE HOENA

Illustrations by LUKE FLOWERS

Music by MARK OBLINGER

CANTATA LEARNING

WWW.CANTATALEARNING.COM

CANTATA
LEARNING

Published by Cantata Learning
1710 Roe Crest Drive
North Mankato, MN 56003
www.cantatalearning.com

A note to educators and librarians from the publisher: Cantata Learning has provided the following data to assist in book processing and suggested use of Cantata Learning product.

Publisher's Cataloging-in-Publication Data
Prepared by Librarian Consultant: Ann-Marie Begnaud
Library of Congress Control Number: 2016938087
    Chuck the Duck Was a Cool Dude : Magic E and the Long U Sound
    Series: Read, Sing, Learn
    By Blake Hoena
    Illustrations by Luke Flowers
    Music by Mark Oblinger
    Summary: The wizard Magic E teaches readers how the silent e changes words like tub to tube, giving them a long U sound, in this outlandish story set to music.
    ISBN: 978-1-63290-792-9 (library binding/CD)
Suggested Dewey and Subject Headings:
    Dewey: E FIC
    LCSH Subject Headings: Wizards – Juvenile literature. | Wizards – Songs and music – Texts. | Wizards – Juvenile sound recording.
    Sears Subject Headings: Magic. | Phonetics. | School songbooks. | Children's songs. | Rock music.
    BISAC Subject Headings: JUVENILE FICTION / Fantasy & Magic. | JUVENILE FICTION / Stories in Verse. | JUVENILE FICTION / Humorous Stories.

Book design and art direction: Tim Palin Creative
Editorial direction: Flat Sole Studio
Music direction: Elizabeth Draper
Music written and produced by Mark Oblinger

Printed in the United States of America in North Mankato, Minnesota.
122016   0339CGS17

ACCESS THE MUSIC!

SCAN CODE WITH MOBILE APP

CANTATALEARNING.COM

TIPS TO SUPPORT LITERACY AT HOME

WHY READING AND SINGING WITH YOUR CHILD IS SO IMPORTANT

Daily reading with your child leads to increased academic achievement. Music and songs, specifically rhyming songs, are a fun and easy way to build early literacy and language development. Music skills correlate significantly with both phonological awareness and reading development. Singing helps build vocabulary and speech development. And reading and appreciating music together is a wonderful way to strengthen your relationship.

READ AND SING EVERY DAY!

TIPS FOR USING CANTATA LEARNING BOOKS AND SONGS DURING YOUR DAILY STORY TIME

1. As you sing and read, point out the different words on the page that rhyme. Suggest other words that rhyme.

2. Memorize simple rhymes such as Itsy Bitsy Spider and sing them together. This encourages comprehension skills and early literacy skills.

3. Use the questions in the back of each book to guide your singing and storytelling.

4. Read the included sheet music with your child while you listen to the song. How do the music notes correlate to the words of the song?

5. Sing along on the go and at home. Access music by scanning the QR code on each Cantata book, or by using the included CD. You can also stream or download the music for free to your computer, smartphone, or mobile device.

Devoting time to daily reading shows that you are available for your child. Together, you are building language, literacy, and listening skills.

Have fun reading and singing!

Have you heard of the Magic E? When added to the end of some words, it changes their vowel sound. For example, *tub* becomes *tube* and **dud** becomes *dude*. Sometimes Magic E is called the Silent E because it does this trick without making a sound.

Now Al-la-ke-zee! Ke-zu-ke-zue! What can the wizard Magic E do with an *E*?

Turn the page to see. Remember to sing along!

Chuck was an odd, odd duck.
Instead of quacking,
he could only cluck, cluck, cluck.

That made him unhappy,
so he went to see
the wizard called Magic E.

"Al-la-ke-zee!
Ke-zu-ke-zue!
With an *E*, I'll turn this dud
into a real cool dude."

Magic E waved his wand,
and with a flick of his wrist—
POOF!
Chuck got a magical gift.

Now Chuck the Duck could quack.

He was proud to make this sound.

But still he felt a **lack**.

He had a dull, gray **hue**.

His feathers were so plain.

But Magic E knew what to do.

"Al-la-ke-zee!
Ke-zu-ke-zue!
With an *E*, I'll turn this **plum**
into a feathery plume."

Magic E waved his wand,
and with a flick of his wrist—
POOF!
Chuck got a magical gift.

Chuck's new look was hip and cool.
With feathers bright as stars,
he **strutted** around the pool.

Quacking Chuck began to **strum** a tune on his **ukulele**.

He sang, "Let's have some fun."

15

"Al-la-ke-zee!
Ke-zu-ke-zue!
With an *E*, I'll turn this tub
into a slippery tube."

Magic E waved his wand,
and with a flick of his wrist—
POOF!
Chuck got a magical gift.

Chuck slid down the slippery tube, flapping and laughing with a new attitude.

When Chuck was through,
he wanted to give
Magic E a big "thank you."

"Al-la-ke-zee!
Ke-zu-ke-zue!
With an *E*, this hug
will become huge."

PLUM
TREE
PLUNGE

Magic E waved his wand,
and with a flick of his wrist—
POOF!
Chuck got a magical gift.

SONG LYRICS
Chuck the Duck Was a Cool Dude

Chuck was an odd, odd duck.
Instead of quacking,
he could only cluck, cluck, cluck.

That made him unhappy,
so he went to see
the wizard called Magic E.

"Al-la-ke-zee!
Ke-zu-ke-zue!
With an E, I'll turn this dud
into a real cool dude."

Magic E waved his wand,
and with a flick of his wrist—
    POOF!
Chuck got a magical gift.

Now Chuck the Duck could quack.
He was proud to make this sound.
But he still felt a lack.

He had a dull, gray hue.
His feathers were so plain.
But Magic E knew what to do.

"Al-la-ke-zee!
Ke-zu-ke-zue!
With an E, I'll turn this plum
into a feathery plume."

Magic E waved his wand,
and with a flick of his wrist—
    POOF!
Chuck got a magical gift.

Chuck's new look was hip and cool.
With feathers bright as stars,
he strutted around the pool.

Quacking Chuck began to strum
a tune on his ukulele.
He sang, "Let's have some fun."

"Al-la-ke-zee!
Ke-zu-ke-zue!
With an E, I'll turn this tub
into a slippery tube."

Magic E waved his wand,
and with a flick of his wrist—
    POOF!
Chuck got a magical gift.

Chuck slid down the slippery tube,
flapping and laughing
with a new attitude.

When Chuck was through,
he wanted to give
Magic E a big "thank you."

"Al-la-ke-zee!
Ke-zu-ke-zue!
With an E, this hug
will become huge."

Magic E waved his wand,
and with a flick of his wrist—
    POOF!
Chuck got a magical gift.

Chuck the Duck Was a Cool Dude

Rock and Roll
Mark Oblinger

Verse

1. Chuck was an odd, odd duck. In-stead of quack-ing, he could on-ly cluck, cluck, cluck. That made him un-hap-py, so he went to see the wiz-ard called Mag-ic E.

Chorus

"Al-la-ke-zee! Ke-zu-ke-zue! With an E, I'll turn this dud in-to a real cool dude." Mag-ic E waved his wand, and with a flick of his wrist— Poof!— Chuck got a mag-i-cal gift.

Verse 2
Now Chuck the Duck could quack.
He was proud to make this sound.
But he still felt a lack.
He had a dull, gray hue.
His feathers were so plain.
But Magic E knew what to do.

Chorus
"Al-la-ke-zee! Ke-zu-ke-zue!
With an E, I'll turn this plum
into a feathery plume."
Magic E waved his wand,
and with a flick of his wrist—
POOF!—
Chuck got a magical gift.

Verse 3
Chuck's new look was hip and cool.
With feathers bright as stars,
he strutted around the pool.
Quacking Chuck began to strum
a tune on his ukulele.
He sang, "Let's have some fun."

Chorus
"Al-la-ke-zee! Ke-zu-ke-zue!
With an E, I'll turn this tub
into a slippery tube."
Magic E waved his wand,
and with a flick of his wrist—
POOF!—
Chuck got a magical gift.

Verse 4
Chuck slid down the slippery tube,
flapping and laughing
with a new attitude.
When Chuck was through,
he wanted to give
Magic E a big "thank you."

Chorus
"Al-la-ke-zee! Ke-zu-ke-zue!
With an E, this hug
will become huge."
Magic E waved his wand,
and with a flick of his wrist—
POOF!—
Chuck got a magical gift.

Outro

GLOSSARY

dud—something that is boring or does not work very well

hue—color

lack—something missing

plum—a small purple or red fruit with a pit

strum—to play a guitar by sweeping your fingers over the strings

strutted—walked with big steps and your head held high

ukulele—a small guitar that is popular in Hawaii

GUIDED READING ACTIVITIES

1. Make a list of words with a long U sound. For example: you, two, few, cute, true, and blue. How many of your words use the Magic E? What are other ways to make a long U sound?

2. Chuck has a friend Luke, a blue mule that plays a flute. Try to draw him.

3. Listen to the song again. Every time you hear a long U sound, stomp your feet. Every time you hear the short U sound, clap your hands.

TO LEARN MORE

Anderson, Steven. *Five Little Ducks*. North Mankato, MN: Cantata Learning, 2016.

Cox, Judy. *Ukulele Hayley*. New York: Holiday House, 2013.

Lefebvre, Jason. *Too Much Glue*. Brooklyn, NY: Flashlight Press, 2013.

London, Jonathan. *Hippos Are Huge!* Somerville, MA: Candlewick Press, 2015.